Fancy NANCY

Halloween... or Bust!

Based on Fancy Nancy written
by Jane O'Connor

Cover illustration by Robin Preiss Glasser

Interior illustrations by Carolyn Bracken

HarperFestival®

A Division of HarperCollins*Publishers*

HarperCollins®, ☰®, and HarperFestival® are trademarks of HarperCollins Publishers.

Fancy Nancy: Halloween . . . or Bust!
Text copyright © 2009 by Jane O'Connor
Illustrations copyright © 2009 by Robin Preiss Glasser
Manufactured in China. All rights reserved. No part of this book may be used or reproduced in any manner whatsoever without written permission except in the case of brief quotations embodied in critical articles and reviews. For information address HarperCollins Children's Books, a division of HarperCollins Publishers, 10 East 53rd Street, New York, NY 10022.
www.harpercollinschildrens.com
Library of Congress cataloging in publication data is available.
ISBN 978-0-06-123595-5

Book design by Sean Boggs
❖
10 11 12 13 LEO 10 9 8 7 6 5 4
First Edition

"Halloween is so much fun," I tell Frenchy,
"because it is all about dressing up.
And that happens to be something I excel at."

On Halloween, you can be...

a caterpillar or

a butterfly...

a glittering silvery snowflake

or a Hollywood movie star ...

DOILIES

or something completely unique.
That's a fancy way of saying one of a kind.

Grrrr

I am a plume-asaurus—a dinosaur that's imaginary.

Even very plain people, like my parents, get fancy on Halloween.

And we must not forget—the bonbons! That's French for candy.

Really, what's not to love?

This year I am going to a Halloween party.
I will be a bunch of grapes
made from fuchsia balloons.

My friend Bree is going as a strawberry.

At the party there are many dazzling costumes.

There are robots

and pirates.

There is even a lion tamer.

Bree's costume has black sequins for strawberry seeds.
"You look spectacular," I tell her.

Bree likes my costume too.
"You even smell grape-y," she says.
"Grape bubble bath," I whisper back.

Soon it is time for games.
First we bob for apples.
It is very hard to do.
I pop four of my balloons.

Next we play pin the tail on the monster.
I bump into Robert's plastic sword
and *pop!* go two more balloons.

By the end of musical chairs,
all of my balloons have popped.

"This is disastrous!" I cry.
That is a fancy way of saying very bad.

Now I am just a brown stalk.
And brown is such a plain color.

But after some punch and many bonbons,
I feel much better.
Then I get a brilliant idea
that is both fancy and smart.

I know who can fix this costume crisis …

...YOU!
Use the stickers to make me a brand-new costume.
And please make it extra fancy.
Merci beaucoup!
(That's French for thanks a bunch.)